This book is for Stan, my youngest grandchild,
With love from AMA

To Máximo —L.L.

About This Book

The illustrations for this book were done in watercolor pencil, Indian ink, acrylic, and digital, with the iPad Pro and Photoshop. This book was edited by Megan Tingley and Anna Prendella and designed by Jen Keenan. The production was supervised by Erika Schwartz, and the production editor was Annie McDonnell. The text was set in Elroy, and the display type is hand-lettered by Jen Keenan.

The Sun Shines Everywhere

By Mary Ann Hoberman

Illustrated by Luciano Lozano

LITTLE, BROWN AND COMPANY

NEW YORK   BOSTON

Some children live in Paris

And others live in Rome.

Some children dwell in New Rochelle

And some call China home.

Some children live in Delhi

And some in Delaware.

It doesn't matter where you live—

The sun shines everywhere!

Some flowers bloom in Fiji
And others bloom in Spain.

Some flowers grow in Tokyo
And others grow in Maine.

Flowers need the rain to grow.

They also need the air,

But mostly they need sunshine, and

The sun shines
everywhere!

It may shine on Earth's other side,

And that is why it's night.

It may be covered by some clouds

And hidden out of sight.

But though we cannot see it,

We know it's always there

Because no matter where we are,

The sun shines everywhere!

Our sun once shone on dinosaurs

And beasts that are no more.

It shone on oceans full of fish

And seashells washed ashore.

It blazed upon the pyramids

And warmed the desert sands.

It spread its rays on Greece and Rome

And other ancient lands.

In feast and famine, peace and war,

It's made its steady way.

Throughout the whole of history

It's never missed a day.

The world is full of animals—

We see some at the zoo—

From pandas off in China

To llamas in Peru.

From crocodiles along the Nile

To growling grizzly bear,

Each creature sees the sun because

The sun shines everywhere!

And even in Antarctica,

Where all the world is white

And ice coats almost everything

And half the year is night,

The patient seals and penguins wait—

They know that even there

The sun will come again because

The sun shines everywhere!

Of course there are some animals

Who spurn the daytime light:

The owls who hoot, the moles who root,

The bats who swoop in flight.

But even if they burrow deep

Or sleep throughout the day,

The foods they eat to keep alive

Need sunshine anyway.

Some children dwell in Switzerland

With mountains all around,

While others dwell in Holland

And live on level ground.

Some children live on islands

Like Cuba or Capri,

While others live far inland

And never see the sea.

So many people in the world,

So many different faces,

So many different languages,

So many different places;

But no matter where we are,

The sun, it doesn't care.

Just wait a while and it will smile.

The sun shines everywhere!

When day is done, there goes the sun

But somewhere day will break.

And while our side is fast asleep

The other side's awake.

The world takes turns at day and night

And each side has its share.

The sun is shining all the time!

The sun shines everywhere!

Everybody needs the sun

To live and grow and thrive.

Our troubles don't feel quite so dark

When sunny days arrive.

No matter what the time of year,

When people see the sun appear,

They start to smile, they're full of cheer

And glad to be alive!